Cat was sleeping in the sun.

Hen looked around the farmyard.

"I have nothing to do," she said.

"I am fed up."

Suddenly, she had an idea.

3

Hen flew up to the top of the hen house.
She took a big breath and shouted,
"Fox! Fox!" as loud as she could.

Cat woke up when she heard Hen shouting.

In a flash, she ran to help.

"Where's the fox?" said Cat.

"I'll scratch him with my claws!"

"Got you!" laughed Hen.

"There isn't a fox, you silly cat.

I had nothing to do, so I played a trick

on you."

"That's not funny," said Cat,

and she went back to lie in the sun.

Hen flew back to the top
of the hen house and looked down.
She saw Dog eating his bone.
She smiled to herself.
"I tricked Cat," she thought.
"Now I will try and trick Dog."

She took a big breath, and cried, "Fox! Fox!"

at the top of her voice.

Dog looked up.

"What's going on?" he said.

He saw Hen on top of the

hen house and went to help.

"Where's the fox?" said Dog.

"My sharp teeth will chew him up!"

"Got you!" laughed Hen.

"There is no fox, you silly dog.

I was fed up, so I played a trick on you."

"Well, I don't think it's very funny," said Dog, and he went back to his bone.

Hen was having so much fun.

Next, she looked down from the hen house

and spotted Ram walking along.

"Fox! Fox!" cried Hen as loud as she could.

Ram ran towards the hen house

to help her.

13

"Where's the fox?" said Ram.

"I'll scare him away with my horns!"

"Got you!" laughed Hen.

"There is no fox, you silly Ram!

It was a trick."

"That's not funny!" said Ram,
and he trotted back to the field.

Hen laughed and laughed at her naughty trick. She was laughing so much that she did not hear Cat, Dog and Ram sneak up behind her. "Fox! Fox!" they all cried.

Hen was so scared that she flew up
to the top of a tree.

"Where's the fox?" said Hen,

flapping her wings.

"Cat, scratch him with your claws.

Dog, chew him up with your sharp teeth.

Ram, scare him away with your horns.

Please don't let him eat me!"

"Got you!" laughed Cat, Dog and Ram.
"There is no fox, you silly hen! You played
a trick on us so we played a trick on you."

From that day on,
Hen never played tricks again.

Story order

Look at these 5 pictures and captions.
Put the pictures in the right order
to retell the story.

1

Dog did not like Hen's trick.

2

Cat ran to help Hen.

3

Cat, Dog and Ram tricked Hen.

4

Ram did not like Hen's trick.

5

Hen was fed up in the farmyard.

Independent Reading

This series is designed to provide an opportunity for your child to read on their own. These notes are written for you to help your child choose a book and to read it independently.

In school, your child's teacher will often be using reading books which have been banded to support the process of learning to read. Use the book band colour your child is reading in school to help you make a good choice. *The Hen Who Cried Fox* is a good choice for children reading at Purple Band in their classroom to read independently.

The aim of independent reading is to read this book with ease, so that your child enjoys the story and relates it to their own experiences.

About the book

Hen is fed up in the farmyard. She decides to play tricks on the other animals by shouting "Fox!" The other animals are not impressed and decide to teach her a lesson.

Before reading

Help your child to learn how to make good choices by asking: "Why did you choose this book? Why do you think you will enjoy it?" Look at the cover together and ask: "What do you think the story will be about?" Ask your child to think of what they already know about the story context. Then ask your child to read the title aloud. Ask: "What would the other animals think when Hen cried Fox?" Remind your child that they can sound out the letters to make a word if they get stuck. Decide together whether your child will read the story independently or read it aloud to you.

During reading

Remind your child of what they know and what they can do independently. If reading aloud, support your child if they hesitate or ask for help by telling the word. If reading to themselves, remind your child that they can come and ask for your help if stuck.

After reading

Support comprehension by asking your child to tell you about the story. Use the story order puzzle to encourage your child to retell the story in the right sequence, in their own words. The correct sequence can be found on the next page.

Help your child think about the messages in the book that go beyond the story and ask: "What lesson do you think the other animals are trying to teach Hen?"

Give your child a chance to respond to the story: "Does this story remind you of any other stories? How do you think Hen felt at the end of the story?"

Extending learning

Help your child predict other possible outcomes of the story by asking: "If Hen kept playing tricks, do you think the other animals would believe her?"

In the classroom, your child's teacher may be teaching how to use speech marks when characters are speaking. There are many examples in this book that you could look at with your child. Find these together and point out how the end punctuation (comma, full stop, question mark or exclamation mark) comes inside the speech marks. Ask the child to read some examples out loud, adding appropriate expression.

Franklin Watts
First published in Great Britain in 2018
by The Watts Publishing Group

Series Editors: Jackie Hamley and Melanie Palmer
Series Advisors: Dr Sue Bodman and Glen Franklin
Series Designer: Peter Scoulding

A CIP catalogue record for this book is
available from the British Library.

ISBN 978 1 4451 6233 1 (hbk)
ISBN 978 1 4451 6235 5 (pbk)
ISBN 978 1 4451 6234 8 (library ebook)

Printed in China

Franklin Watts
An imprint of
Hachette Children's Group
Part of The Watts Publishing Group
Carmelite House
50 Victoria Embankment
London EC4Y 0DZ

An Hachette UK Company
www.hachette.co.uk

www.franklinwatts.co.uk

Answer to Story order: 5, 2, 1, 4, 3